Dear Parents:

Congratulations! Your child is taking the first steps on an exciting journey. The destination? Independent reading!

STEP INTO READING® will help your child get there. The program offers five steps to reading success. Each step includes fun stories and colorful art or photographs. In addition to original fiction and books with favorite characters, there are Step into Reading Non-Fiction Readers, Phonics Readers and Boxed Sets, Sticker Readers, and Comic Readers—a complete literacy program with something to interest every child.

Learning to Read, Step by Step!

Ready to Read   Preschool–Kindergarten
• big type and easy words • rhyme and rhythm • picture clues
For children who know the alphabet and are eager to begin reading.

Reading with Help   Preschool–Grade 1
• basic vocabulary • short sentences • simple stories
For children who recognize familiar words and sound out new words with help.

Reading on Your Own   Grades 1–3
• engaging characters • easy-to-follow plots • popular topics
For children who are ready to read on their own.

Reading Paragraphs   Grades 2–3
• challenging vocabulary • short paragraphs • exciting stories
For newly independent readers who read simple sentences with confidence.

Ready for Chapters   Grades 2–4
• chapters • longer paragraphs • full-color art
For children who want to take the plunge into chapter books but still like colorful pictures.

STEP INTO READING® is designed to give every child a successful reading experience. The grade levels are only guides; children will progress through the steps at their own speed, developing confidence in their reading.

Remember, a lifetime love of reading starts with a single step!

Copyright © 2019 Disney Enterprises, Inc. All rights reserved. Published in the United States by Random House Children's Books, a division of Penguin Random House LLC, 1745 Broadway, New York, NY 10019, and in Canada by Penguin Random House Canada Limited, Toronto, in conjunction with Disney Enterprises, Inc.

Step into Reading, Random House, and the Random House colophon are registered trademarks of Penguin Random House LLC.

Visit us on the Web!
StepIntoReading.com
rhcbooks.com

Educators and librarians, for a variety of teaching tools, visit us at RHTeachersLibrarians.com

ISBN 978-0-7364-3951-0 (trade) — ISBN 978-0-7364-8268-4 (lib. bdg.)
ISBN 978-0-7364-3952-7 (ebook)

Printed in the United States of America   10 9 8 7 6 5 4 3 2 1

Random House Children's Books supports the First Amendment and celebrates the right to read.

DUMBO

by Christy Webster

illustrated by Francesco Legramandi

Random House 🏠 New York

Casey Jr. is
a circus train.

On board are bears,
hippos, tigers,
and . . .

elephants!

One day,
the stork arrives.

He brings
a baby elephant.
Mrs. Jumbo is happy.

Dumbo is

the smallest elephant . . .

with the biggest ears!

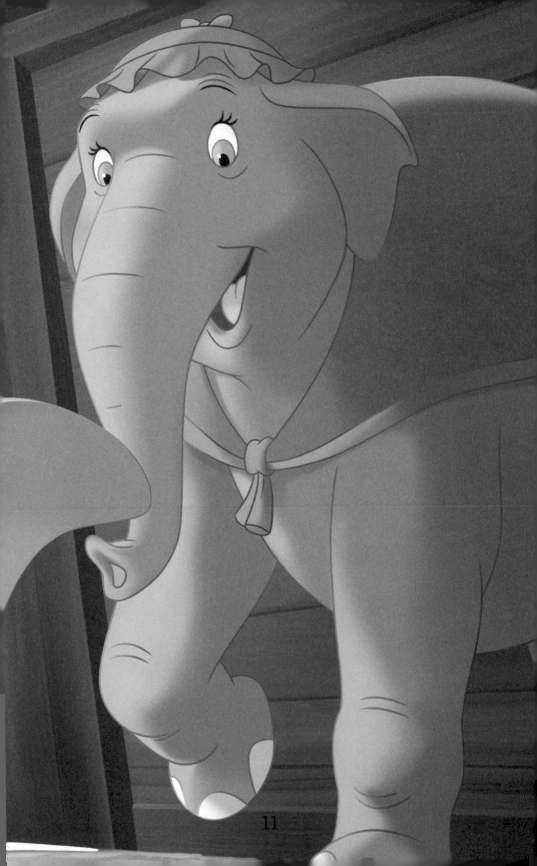

Dumbo joins
the show.
He trips
over his ears.

Everyone laughs.

Dumbo is sad.

Timothy the mouse
is Dumbo's friend.

He wants

to cheer Dumbo up.

Timothy gives Dumbo
a magic feather.

With the magic feather,
Dumbo can fly!

At the next show,
the feather slips away.

But Dumbo believes.

He still flies!

Mrs. Jumbo and Timothy
are proud of Dumbo.

Dumbo is a star!